DREAMWORKS

VOLTRON
LEGENDARY DEFENDER

Shiro's Story

By Cala Spinner

Illustrated by Patrick Spaziante

Ready-to-Read

Simon Spotlight
New York London Toronto Sydney New Delhi

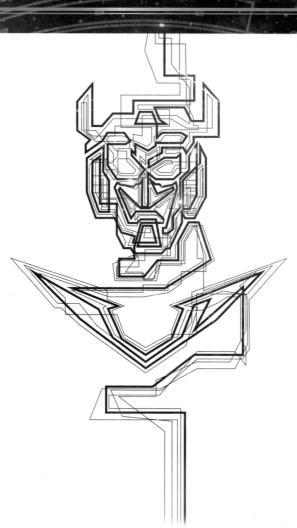

SIMON SPOTLIGHT
An imprint of Simon & Schuster Children's Publishing Division
1230 Avenue of the Americas, New York, New York 10020
This Simon Spotlight edition May 2018
Manufactured in the United States of America 0318 LAK
2 4 6 8 10 9 7 5 3 1
ISBN 978-1-5344-1831-8 (hc)
ISBN 978-1-5344-1830-1 (pbk)
ISBN 978-1-5344-1832-5 (eBook)

My name is Shiro.
This is the story of how
I became the leader of Voltron.
Voltron is a robotic warrior
made of five lions and five pilots.
Its pilots are called Paladins.
I pilot the Black Lion.

Before I became a Paladin,
I learned how to be a pilot
at a school on Earth.
It is called the Galaxy Garrison.

At the Garrison,
I met a student
named Matt Holt.
He wanted to be the
first human to meet aliens.

After we finished school, Matt and I were selected by his father, Sam, to go on an important mission. We were told to travel to Kerberos, one of Pluto's moons, and collect signs of alien life.

I was excited.
We were going to fly farther
than any pilot had ever gone
before!

After we landed on Kerberos,
Matt and his father began
to collect ice samples
to study.

But then disaster struck.

A fleet of aliens found us
and forced us onto their ship.
They called themselves the Galra.
We became their prisoners.

The Galra sent Matt's father away. They made Matt and me become fighters in their arena.

Matt was supposed to fight first,
but I knew he wasn't ready.
I needed to protect my friend,
so I did the one thing
I could think of.
I injured him so he couldn't fight.

Because of what I did,
the Galra had to send me to fight
instead of Matt.
In the arena, I never lost a battle.
The Galra started calling me
the Champion.

Then an alien witch named Haggar
gave me a robotic arm.
She wanted me to become
a weapon for the Galra.

I had no idea that a Galra rebel was watching from a distance.

His name was Ulaz.
Ulaz did not like
the Galra Empire.
He knew the Galra were looking
for a weapon called Voltron,
and he didn't want them to find it.

Ulaz believed part of Voltron
was hidden on Earth.
He helped me escape.
I traveled back to Earth and
warned everyone that
the Galra were coming.

But when I returned,
no one listened to me.
My hair had changed and
my new robotic arm scared them.
They wanted to run some tests.

Then an old friend of mine
named Keith came to my rescue.
Three other Garrison students,
Hunk, Lance, and Pidge, came too.

We escaped to Keith's
secret hiding place.
Keith had been researching
a strange energy nearby.
We followed the energy and found
a cave with a spaceship inside.
It was blue and shaped like a lion!

The lion opened up for Lance.
He became its pilot!
We all climbed on board
and flew into space.
The spaceship flew so fast,
we passed Kerberos in seconds!

The lion took us to a planet
called Arus.

There we met two new aliens,
Princess Allura and her
advisor, Coran.
They helped us find
the other four lion spaceships.
We needed all five lions to
form Voltron.

I bonded with the Black Lion.
This made me the leader of Voltron.
Allura said that the Black Lion
needs a pilot who is in control
at all times.

Becoming a Paladin of Voltron
has taught me a lot about
what it means to be a leader.

Being a leader means that
I have to use my instincts.

For example, when Allura didn't
believe that Ulaz's team was
on our side, I stepped in.
My instinct was to trust them.
It led to a powerful alliance.

Sometimes being a leader means
working hard instead of relaxing.

It also means training while
the other Paladins have fun.

Being a Defender of the Universe
isn't easy, but it is important.
I like to say that
"patience yields focus."
One day I hope that patience
will help us defeat the Galra,
once and for all!